CONTENTS

Army recruits must endure extensive training to meet strict requirements. You should consider all the pros and cons of army life before you decide to join this branch of the U.S. armed forces.

CHAPTER ONE

THINKING IT OVER

He's rude, nasty, unfair and he doesn't know when to stop. He makes you do the same thing over and over until you do it without thinking.

You don't like him at all. That's all right with him. He's just doing his job: making sure you learn how to survive under enemy fire. Lots of soldiers have felt the same way you do. But in Korea, Vietnam and the Persian Gulf, they thanked their lucky stars he had been tough on them.

So meet one of the most important people in your army career—your drill instructor. You probably feel as though you already know him. After all, he's a stock character in every army movie you've ever seen.

All drill instructors have the rank of sergeant. You won't see your drill sergeant until you start the **basic training** portion of your **Initial Entry Training**. Before that day arrives, you will have made some very important decisions.

You may think joining the army seems like a good idea. But there are almost as many reasons for signing up—or not signing up—as there are soldiers. First ask yourself, "Is the army right for me?" Nobody can make that decision for you.

Before deciding, carefully examine all your reasons why and why not. A great deal depends on you as a person, what you like to do and what your dreams and interests are.

On the positive side, you may want a job that promises action. Living in a foreign country for a short period in peacetime sounds exciting. Perhaps you do not have any job skills and you want to earn money while you learn. The skills you are taught in the army may help you later when you enter the civilian job market. You may hope to continue your schooling. The army will help you with that. You receive pay while on vacation and you don't have to worry about doctors' bills. You may think it's cool to live away from home and make new friends. A steady paycheck sounds pretty good too. Or it may be pride in serving your country.

If these things are what you are looking for in life, the army may be right for you.

On the negative side, you may find it hard that decisions are made that affect your life and you have nothing to say about them. This can be very upsetting. You have to go where the army tells you, even if you hate the place. Orders must not be questioned. It isn't like living at home, where you may be able to wiggle out of doing something you're supposed to do. You may find yourself working at a job you detest with people you'd never pick as friends. You can't quit, at least not until your enlistment is up. If you live on an army **base**, you may feel trapped and that you have no freedom. If these things would make you miserable, the army is probably not for you.

List what you like about the army and what you do not like. Then talk it over with your school counselor. Your school

As an army trainee, you should be prepared to follow directions and carry out orders.

counselor knows your school record and knows about you from your teachers. He or she will tell you that in order to enlist, you must contact an army **recruiter**. The counselor may offer to be present at your initial meeting with the recruiter or suggest that your parents be involved. The U.S. Army recruiter will review your records and tell you if you qualify to join the U.S. Army.

Always remember, being a soldier is not the same as camping out or going for a hike in the mountains. It's a very serious business.

The army offers many jobs and opportunities to fit a wide range of skills and interests. If you play a musical instrument, you may want to consider joining the army band.

CHAPTER TWO

THE ASVAB

As an 18-year-old male, you obeyed the law and registered at the post office. This is required so that the federal government will know how many young men are available for a draft in time of an emergency.

Your school days are almost over. By now your counselor knows you are thinking of joining the army. You will be told you must take a test, the **Armed Services Vocational Aptitude Battery (ASVAB).** This test is given at high schools. If your school doesn't give the ASVAB, a recruiter will let you know about taking it at another testing place. It's good to take this test even if you don't become a soldier. From your score your future employer will learn what work you are best fitted for. The answers you give to the test's questions guide the army in knowing where to assign you. This means matching a job that interests you with work that you can do successfully.

During basic training you will meet and work alongside many other new recruits. Some of these recruits will probably become your closest friends.

The U.S. Army offers challenging and rewarding positions to both male and female recruits. This woman is being trained in the field of communications.

Teamwork is an important aspect of army life, so you should be sure that you are able to work well with others before enlisting.

Even more important is what you can learn about yourself from the ASVAB. You may discover a talent you did not realize you have. Ask your counselor to discuss your test scores with you. Some schools ask an army recruiter to come in and explain the results of the tests. Use this information to prepare yourself for the future.

The ASVAB tries to find out what you know about arithmetic, the meaning of certain words, auto and shop information, understanding of mechanics and lots of other subjects.

A sample arithmetic question: "How many 36-passenger buses will it take to carry 144 passengers?" You have a choice of one out of four answers: "3," "4," "5," "6." Figured it out?

A word-meaning sample: "The wind is *variable* today." Pick which of the following is correct: "mild," "steady," "shifting," "chilling."

Don't worry if you are weak in some subjects. The army doesn't expect you to know everything! You can study for this test, just as you can for a school exam. The library has books to help you, including sample tests.

It is possible to flunk. After 30 days you can try again. If you fail this second time, you have to wait six months. (It costs the army about $180 each time you take the ASVAB.)

Army soldiers may encounter enemy attacks without warning. Before signing up, ask yourself how well you react to dangerous situations.

CHAPTER THREE

ASKING QUESTIONS

You're worried. What if the recruiter tries to get you to enlist even if you're not sure? A recruiter is not supposed to pressure you into joining, but it does happen. To be a recruiter, a soldier has to have been in the army a long time, served many **hitches** (reenlistments) and reached the rank of sergeant. Those assigned to that duty have pride in the military force in which they serve.

Although some will urge you to join, don't be pushed into signing until you are absolutely sure you want to be a soldier. That is very important—for you, for your future and for the army too. Sadly, some recruiters have been known not to be entirely truthful with people wanting information about joining the army. One 20-year-old enlistee claims the recruiter told him "a bunch of lies." Others say they were not told the truth about the jobs they'd be doing, about the length of time overseas and about how to get the bonus the army offers for enlisting in certain branches.

Don't be afraid to ask questions. Pick up all the brochures you can find. Say you wish to see videos of army life. Always keep in mind that life is never as easy as it seems on the screen.

Surprised that the recruiter answers some questions before you ask? No, it's not mind reading. Recruiters learn what you want to know. One of the questions most often asked by male **recruits** is "Do I have to have my hair cut?" Yes! Definitely! No matter that it's your pride and joy, that it already ends above your shoulders, an army barber will cut it.

Another frequently asked question is "Can I take my car to basic training?" No! First, there would not be enough parking space if all recruits brought their cars. Second, you will have no free time to go off the base during your eight weeks of basic training. Also, you will be so tired you will fall gratefully into bed each night. Even driving a car will seem like too much work!

Some of the questions you plan to ask are simple, such as, "Who can join the army? For how long? Do you have to be a high school graduate?"

Others can be answered only by someone who really knows. An example: "Do I really have to sign a paper? What do I agree to when I sign up?"

The simple questions first. Who can join? Any man or woman, married or single, between the ages of 17 and 34. If you are 17, you must have the consent of a parent or guardian. Bring your birth certificate and social security card with you. If you don't have either, you need proof of your birth date and that you are a United States citizen.

Army recruits are trained on military equipment to fight off enemies that might threaten the United States or its interests.

If your parents are American and lived out of the country when you were born, you have to show proof of citizenship. If your parents are *not* Americans and you were *not* born in the United States, you will be asked to prove that you came into this country lawfully for permanent residency (a green card).

If you have decided you really want to join, bring those papers with you when you enlist in the army.

17

CHAPTER FOUR

AND STILL MORE QUESTIONS

You should be thinking over how long you want to stay in the army. Of course, a lot depends on how well you get along. But you should be deciding whether for your first stint you will sign up for two, four or six years **active service**. After your first enlistment you are free to leave the service or to reenlist.

Regardless of how long you sign up for active service, you are actually joining for a total of eight years. It works like this: You want to be a soldier for six years. That is the length of time you are on active duty. The remaining two years you are in the **inactive reserve.** If you sign up for four years, you'll spend four years in the inactive reserve. Two years active service will leave you with six years in the inactive reserve. Inactive

(Photo left)   As a member of the army, you will acquire skills that can later be applied to civilian jobs.

reservists have no army duties. You return to civilian life. In case of war, however, you may be recalled to active service.

Although both men and women can enlist, there are some differences. If you are a man, the army wants you to graduate from high school, so check with a recruiter before you decide to drop out.

If you're a woman, that's not the case. Then you *must* have a high school diploma. (The marines and air force also have this requirement for women.)

For your future, far more important are the facts about military service the recruiter will discuss with you.

Your ASVAB results have told the army what jobs you can do successfully. In times of peace the government promises to place you in work you want and can be trained to do. This hinges on two things: your ability to really do that job and whether there is an opening in that area.

Sometimes the army is short of people in certain branches. If you enlist in one of them, you will be given extra money. This sum varies. Depending on the branch, it ranges from $2,000 to $8,000. These amounts can and do change as the needs of the army vary.

There are over 300 skills needed to run the army. You may have a job skill the army can use. What about driving? Truck drivers may be in short supply. Play a musical instrument? Give the army band a thought. Ever work in a restaurant? Think about food service—the army has to eat too!

If you have a skill the army can use and there is an opening in that branch, you can enter at a higher grade and earn more pay right from the start. You'll skip the first two **ranks** and begin your army career as a **private** first class. (You still have to go to basic training.)

Action is what you want. "No more education," you say. You've had it with the classroom. Two or four or six years from now, you may change your mind. Ask the recruiter. He'll explain the various ways you can get financial help from the army. Some have to be applied for when you enlist. No harm in asking!

During the summer of 1991, the Congress of the United States reversed its stand on women serving in combat units.

Looking for adventure? There are many action-oriented jobs needed to run the army. Check with your recruiter to see which ones you might be most qualified for.

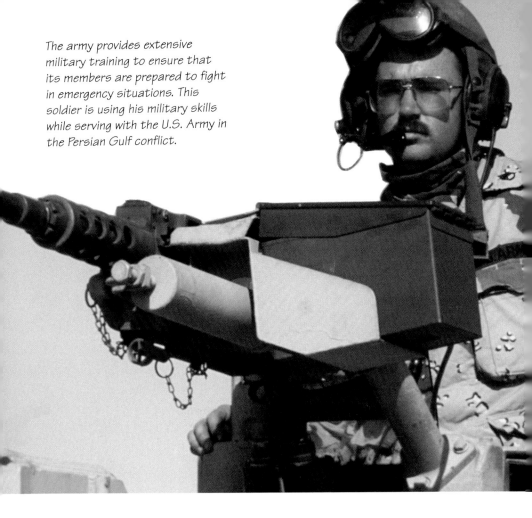

The army provides extensive military training to ensure that its members are prepared to fight in emergency situations. This soldier is using his military skills while serving with the U.S. Army in the Persian Gulf conflict.

Until then, women were not permitted in fighting areas. In the Persian Gulf conflict, many women flew in cargo planes and helped evacuate soldiers from the war zone. Under the new law, women may not be sent to any area where hand-to-hand combat is likely to occur.

Other questions float through your mind. You saw a picture of some guys wearing jaunty red berets. What do they do? They're **paratroopers**, infantrymen who jump from airplanes—behind enemy lines in wartime. The infantry does a lot more today than slug through mud and camp out in the rain. Mechanized units even ride inside armored personnel carriers.

Rangers are also in the infantry. They undergo special intensive training, including six days with only 16 hours of sleep while they climb cliffs and learn to survive in boiling desert heat and humid jungles. It's tough and rugged.

"Can I become an army pilot?" you ask. As an enlisted soldier, only if you qualify for helicopter training. A recruiter can tell you what's required.

If any doubts remain with you about joining the army, now is the time to discuss them. Go home and think it over. But if you are sure, then you will be asked to sign an application form at the recruiting station. This merely lets the government know you want to join the army. Signing the form is *not* enlisting.

As an enlisted soldier, you will have an opportunity to learn all about the complicated machinery and military equipment used in the U.S. Army.

CHAPTER FIVE

SIGNING UP

So you've decided—it's the army for you! But do you qualify? Will the army take you?

No matter what job you apply for in life, it's the employer who has the final say. The army is no different, though the army wants to know more about you than employers usually do. True, most of the questions center on your background, but your interests and hopes are also discussed.

Be honest. If you don't tell the truth, the army will find out. A felony conviction will result in your being turned down, and so will a drug problem. Receiving six or more traffic tickets in one year will make it hard for you to convince the army you are eager to obey the law and accept responsibility. And you must pass a very thorough physical examination at the **Military Entrance Processing Station (MEPS).**

Once you have signed the application form, the recruiter will arrange for you to go to a MEPS. These Processing Stations are scattered throughout the country in large cities. If there isn't one near you, the army will pay for your trip and even put you up in a hotel the night before you enlist. If you live close enough, you can get there on your own or be driven to it by a recruiter.

It will be a long day. At the hotel, wake-up time may be 3:30 A.M. (the time may vary from one station to another). Whether at the hotel or at home, you must shower and put on clean clothes. If wake-up time is 3:30 A.M. breakfast will be served at 4:00 A.M., you're then expected in the hotel lobby by 5:00 A.M. and from there you will be taken to the MEPS. All applicants (men and women for all the armed forces) will be gathered there between 5:00 and 5:30 A.M.

Once there, not every applicant does the same thing at the same time. For instance, have you taken the ASVAB? If not, today's the day you will.

For most, the first event is the physical, the only time men and women are separated. Don't forget to bring along copies of your medical records. The army wants to know if you've had major surgery, a serious illness or any broken bones. A small sample of blood will be taken to test you for HIV, the virus that causes AIDS.

You may never have realized that you're color-blind. That won't keep you out, but it will eliminate you from any job in which wires or parts are color coded. Your mistaking a red wire for a green might be fatal to someone using that piece of equipment.

You will be tested for alcohol and drug use. Your weight will be taken to be sure it is within the limits the service has set

Interested in flying? You may qualify for army helicopter training.

for your height. Conditions such as asthma or curvature of the spine will keep you out of the army.

After turning in the paperwork and the results of your physical to a guidance counselor, you'll head for the **Entrance National Agency Checks (ENTNAC)**. You will be interviewed and fingerprinted. This is to be sure you are not a security risk to the country. Here's another chance to update your application form, in case you forgot to answer some of the questions. This time you *must* answer all of them.

By now you're starving. Lunch is free at the MEPS. Going outside to eat may be okay, but you'll have to pay for it yourself.

It's time for an interview with an army guidance counselor. Your test and school grades are important in his or her evaluation of your choice of career.

Together you and the counselor will study a computer printout. Job options are listed for you to consider, and the counselor will help you choose. Of course, you may already know what you want to do. If your testing proves you are capable of doing that kind of work, there should be no problem.

Don't settle for a career skill that doesn't interest you merely because there is no opening in your choice. If you hope to be an air traffic controller, don't agree to become a truck driver because that's the only opening. Just delay your active service and return to MEPS again and again, until you get the job you want and are qualified to do. Become part of the army's **Delayed Entry Program**.

Once you have signed with the army, your job choice usually cannot be changed. You have to wait until your enlistment is up and then reenlist to change your job. The army may ask you to switch to another job for various reasons, such as your unit being reduced in personnel. That does not happen very often.

So be doubly sure your job choice is listed correctly before you write your name on the contract. It is a legally binding contract.

Now you are ready to take the oath. You will repeat the same words many famous people have spoken, including Presidents Jimmy Carter, Ronald Reagan, Lyndon Johnson, George Bush and Dwight Eisenhower. Among other well-

The United States Military Academy in West Point, New York, is the oldest military college in the nation. Here, young men and women prepare for careers as officers in the U.S. Army.

known people who have taken that same oath are Elvis Presley, Norman Schwarzkopf and America's astronauts, including Sally Ride.

Swearing-in is a very solemn moment, when you pledge yourself to defend your country. Then your photo is taken, and you walk out the door an enlistee.

Officially, you're in the army. Next step: reporting for duty.

CHAPTER SIX

YOU'RE IN THE ARMY NOW

Once more you're on a trip, courtesy of the army. This time to basic training, the first portion of Initial Entry Training. Just where you go depends on what you've signed up to do: Infantry, you're headed for Fort Benning, Georgia; Armor (tanks), you're going to Fort Knox, Kentucky; in Field **Artillery** your destination is Fort Sill, Oklahoma; Air Defense trains at Fort Bliss, Texas; Combat Engineers at Fort Leonard Wood, Missouri; and Military Police at Fort McClellan, Alabama. Each of these sites is known as **One Station Unit Training**, where basic combat training and **Advanced Individual Training (AIT)** in these skills are given.

Soldiers assigned to other jobs must also attend basic training for eight weeks before moving to AIT. The same course is required for both men and women.

(Photo left) You will not need to do much packing for basic training. The army will supply you with the uniforms that you are required to wear.

How you react to basic training depends to a large degree on how you approach it. It's vital for you to realize there's a reason for the tough time you're having during these first eight weeks (plus three days). Sometime in the future, what you learn at basic may save your life. Just as in training for the Olympics, you want to stay on the good side of the coach, so in the army you want to avoid having a falling-out with your drill sergeant.

These weeks at basic are similar to getting in shape for a game. You may feel the coach—or drill sergeant—is picking on you, that you're trying hard to please but he or she doesn't appreciate you. Many times you feel like quitting (in the army you can't!) but you stick it out and then that big day comes when you graduate and go on to AIT.

Recruits are organized into **squads**, usually of ten people, with a sergeant in command. Several squads form a **platoon**. Three or more platoons make up a **company**. Then comes a **battalion** of four to six companies. Several battalions are gathered into a **brigade**, and then a **division**, commanded by a general and made up of battalions and brigades. At the beginning all you are concerned with is your own squad, platoon and company. There are approximately 220 people in a company.

That first night in your bunk, you're frightened. You've heard wild stories about how horrible basic is. The army still seems like a good idea to you but now you begin to wonder...

Everyone in your **barracks** is probably having the same doubts you are. Each of them is just as nervous about the sudden change from civilian to military life.

One recruit, his first night in the army, stood at attention by his bunk as the sergeant came down the aisle. "Name?" he barked. The recruit was so nervous he couldn't remember his own name! Just remember, you are not alone.

Your army drill sergeant will work to put you in the best physical shape possible during basic training.

This may be the first time you are treated like an adult; it is for many. You are expected to be responsible for your possessions, for paying your bills and for shining your boots. No one is there to do it for you.

International law requires that you wear a uniform. Within 72 hours of arrival at basic, you receive yours. These first days will be spent just standing in line—or so it seems to you. You stand in line to pick up your clothing, collect equipment (some of which you can't identify) and wait hungrily for meals.

You listen to lectures about pay-saving plans, health benefits and insurance. Then you will spend some time taking tests in an effort by the army to learn more about your abilities. No grades involved! Usually, on the third day, you receive immunization shots. And men, don't forget the famous haircut given by an army barber. You'll look in the mirror, see yourself and wonder who the stranger is!

Women, you've got it better! All you have to make sure is that your hair clears your collar. The army wants you to look your best; after all, you represent the United States wherever you go. So part of your basic training is a course on how to apply makeup.

Usually, on day four begins the actual military training. Among the many subjects you are taught are first aid, how to salute properly (and when to), survival under combat, field sanitation, personal hygiene, drills and ceremonies, army history and weapons instruction including all types of **grenades** and the M16 rifle. You start the day at 5:30 A.M. and are kept busy until lights-out at 9:30 P.M.

The most important thing you learn is to obey orders—or else! For some, that's the hardest part of basic training. Don't question. Just do what you're told. Never get on the wrong side of your sergeant!

Be prepared to be yelled at, insulted and called names; to march until you think your feet will fall off and do push-ups until your elbows feel like melting popsicles; to clean **latrines**, wash floors and do KP (kitchen police), which means peeling enough potatoes and chopping enough carrots for—well, an army!

Also be prepared to go on **bivouac** (camping out) in rain, hail or sunshine; become an acrobat to finish an obstacle course; learn to take apart an M16 rifle and put it together again; survive a live ammunition exercise and gasp for breath in a

34

poison gas drill. It is important you know how to live through battle conditions.

Although both sexes train at the same camp and go through the same tough routine, they have their own barracks and don't train together. A woman may find herself with a male drill sergeant, just as a man may find himself taking orders from a female drill sergeant.

Have you ever done something—say, taken a roller coaster ride—and hated every minute of it, only to find when it's over that you enjoyed it? That's basic for some. One recruit claims she cried every night but looking back, she thinks basic was a lot of fun. Another says all recruits are treated like animals! It all depends on you and your attitude.

It isn't easy. The army admits it's tough. The aim is to make you a part of a team. When you finish basic, you'll be in better physical shape than you've ever been.

Graduation day you march with your company, a surge of pride rushing through you. You take your place in a long line of volunteer soldiers, beginning with the militia, formed by early settlers for their protection, and followed by the minutemen, who fought in the American Revolution. Although the United States has periodically had a draft to enlist men to fight a war, one of the main strengths of the United States has been its volunteer army.

Now you're ready to move on to AIT.

CHAPTER SEVEN

AIT AND BEYOND

During AIT you receive specialized training in your chosen career. If you were assigned to a One Station Unit Training, you'll stay where you are with a one-day leave to transfer your belongings from one barracks to another. If not, the next nine weeks will be spent at another army base. Your AIT may not be scheduled to start immediately. If that happens, you'll have a leave until your AIT begins.

Signed up to become a paratrooper? Fort Bragg, North Carolina, will be your new home. Hope to work for the telephone company someday so you enlisted in the Signal Corps? You head for Fort Monmouth, New Jersey. Want to be a butcher? You're on your way to the Meat and Dairy Hygiene School in Chicago, Illinois.

In some ways, it's similar to basic. You still live in barracks, march with your squad to and from classes and are without a car. The mess hall remains your dining room.

If you've signed up to become a paratrooper, you will be trained to jump from airplanes behind enemy lines in wartime at Fort Bragg, North Carolina.

There are differences too. Men and women train together and squads are made up of both sexes. You sing in **cadence** as you jog as long as your sergeant feels like it. AIT is not as hard on you physically. It's more like going to school, but you're only taught what you need to know to do a good job in the skill you've chosen.

The biggest difference is that discipline is less strict. The sergeant is not as tough on you. You begin to feel more like a soldier.

Basic and AIT are over, and you're ready for your first **tour of duty**. Tour of duty is the term used for the amount of time a soldier is assigned to a specific place. Most times it lasts four years.

Where will your first tour of duty be? Maybe overseas. The army is changing, and being sent out of the country for your first tour is not as sure as it once was. Congress isn't spending as much money to run the army as it used to, and many bases, both overseas and at home, are being closed. The chances are still pretty good that you will spend some of your active service years in a foreign country.

You're ready for action. Even in peacetime you'll be kept busy. Perhaps you're in the **Quartermaster Corps**. Ordering supplies is vital for the army's survival—and don't forget the eggs for breakfast! Maybe you're in the Corps of Engineers. That branch is responsible for the building of bridges, inland waterways and roads. You might find yourself working on a dredge on the Mississippi River. You're interested in law. The Judge Advocate's office may need a clerk—how's your typing? Or you want to get on with your job in the Military Police.

Life will settle down to a more normal routine of getting up, going to work (even if that means driving a tank!) and then, after work, being free to do as you want. You report for the same 40-hour workweek as a civilian. Remember, though, that you are a soldier and may be assigned working hours at any time of day or night (you might even pull guard duty!) or unexpectedly be put on alert.

The routine is broken also when you go on **maneuvers**, a practice battle in which you are able to use the skills you have acquired at basic and AIT.

Whether your tour of duty is overseas or stateside, you probably live on the base and, if unmarried, still sleep in a barracks. Most army installations are like small towns, with many ways to spend your free time. Not every base has everything, but most have a movie theater, gym, swimming pool, snack bar and library.

You're thinking of getting married. Where will you live? If there is an opening in the married housing facility, you might stay on base. If not, you'll move off the base and receive a basic allowance for **quarters** (BAQ), quarters being the military name for your housing. Sometimes you may be assigned to a place in which it is expensive to live. You'll be given an extra cost-of-living allowance.

Now you start to wonder when you'll be promoted and get an increase in pay. In basic and AIT you are a private without any insignia on your sleeve. After six months of active service and with the commander's approval, you'll be promoted to private **(E-2)**, receive more pay and sew a chevron on your sleeve.

Each increase in rank is done by the same method: length of time in service, actual time in rank, how well you're doing and the commander's approval. That means to go from private first class **(E-3)** to corporal **(E-4)**, you must have served actively for 24 months, and for six of those months you must have been a private first class **(E-3)**.

This is one reason to change your mind about education. For all ranks from corporal **(E-4)** on up to sergeant major of the army **(E-9)**, the highest you can go without being a commissioned **officer**, you must have a high school diploma.

Passing a physical training test, a weapons test and a **Skill Qualification Test** are also required for promotion.

By using the **Army Continuing Education System**, you can work toward a higher rank by studying. Talk to your sergeant. You'll be surprised at the many ways the army will help you. And when the time comes for the yearly review of your work, it will look good on your record.

Army soldiers are trained to defend themselves as well as their fellow soldiers in wartime.

CHAPTER EIGHT

FULL-TIME VS. PART-TIME ARMY LIFE

"If you can't make friends in the army, you can't make friends," claims one ex-tank driver.

Soldiers are a friendly group. You all start out equal in basic training. You share experiences. In those first weeks you become a team, eager to help one another. If an enlistee doesn't get the hang of squaring the blankets on his or her bunk, one of you shows him or her how. You get after the one who doesn't keep his or her boots polished, who brings down the anger of the drill sergeant on your squad. You are bonded into a unit of which you are proud.

From then on, wherever you serve, you make friends. If you stay in the army long enough, you discover someone you knew years before during a different tour of duty, now at the same post. It's almost like belonging to a club.

Perhaps you think it would be fun to be in the army but you don't want to spend every day at it, not even for just two years. The **active army reserve** may be the answer.

Age and other requirements are the same for joining the active army reserve as for enlisting in the regular army. Basic is done over two summers or all at once during one summer. Reservists go on to AIT, which usually lasts eight weeks. For your training you are paid full army pay. Although you are a civilian, you must meet with a unit for 16 hours a month (one weekend or two eight-hour days). In addition, you spend two weeks keeping up with new techniques and reviewing what you learned in basic and AIT.

After becoming an army reservist, you can enlist in the regular army without worrying about basic training; you've already done it. The same holds true of AIT unless you change your **Military Occupational Specialty (MOS)**. Then you go through AIT in your new career choice.

Remember, this is the *active* army reserve, not the *inactive*. You must already have served some years in active service to be in the inactive reserve. The inactive reserve was explained in chapter four.

There is another way of experiencing army life. The **Army National Guard** combines activities of both the federal government and the state. During emergencies, such as an earthquake, hurricane or any natural disaster, you will be called upon to keep order, stop looting and rescue victims. It's a state army. During a war it usually is attached to the regular army. The same requirements exist for joining, although a ninth-grade education is required. You'll receive full pay when on duty.

After you've been in the army—regular, active reserve or the National Guard—you may decide you'd like to become an officer. In all cases talk it over with your sergeant. Or before you enlist, get the information from your recruiter.

During basic training you will learn the importance of cooperation. This knowledge will be of great use to you throughout your army career.

At the end of each enlistment, you have two choices: reenlist or retire from the army. It all depends on how much you like or dislike army life. Some soldiers rebel at the discipline, at the loss of control of their lives, at always having to obey orders, at being passed over for promotion. Others enjoy the job security, the moving, the benefits, the learning of a skill, the friendships.

Those who follow through with the difficult training and requirements of the army usually become strong men and women who are proud to represent and defend their country.

One ex-tank driver says, "I'm glad I was in the army. It gave me self-confidence." Others feel bullied, trapped by having Military Police guard the entrance of the base.

The decision to enlist or not to enlist is up to you. Nobody can make up your mind for you. Move carefully. Consider the yes reasons. Think over the no reasons.

Whatever career you choose—in the army or out—you know you have considered many of the pros and cons of army life.

GLOSSARY

active army reserve A member of the active reserve is a
civilian who serves part-time in the army but has a regular
full-time job.

active service As a member of the active service, the army
is your only job. You are a full-time soldier.

Advanced Individual Training (AIT) Training received in
your job specialty after finishing recruit training.

Armed Services Vocational Aptitude Battery (ASVAB) A
test required of all those who hope to join one of the armed
services.

Army Continuing Education System Ways in which the
army will help you continue your studies.

Army National Guard A way of serving part-time that
combines the activities of both the federal government
(army) and of your home state. Its members are called out
during national emergencies and natural disasters (flood,
earthquake), wherever and whenever damage is large.

artillery Large guns and cannons that fire a long distance.

barracks Building in which you sleep and keep your possessions.

base Government-owned property or property being used
by one of the armed services.

basic training Your first training after you report for duty. During basic training, you learn how to be an army soldier.

battalion A unit composed of four to six companies.

bivouac Camping out, with and without tents.

brigade A unit composed of several battalions.

cadence Rhythm (as in marching).

company Three or more platoons (approximately 220 people).

Delayed Entry Program A program for putting off (delaying) your reporting for active service after you have enlisted.

division An army unit made up of battalions and brigades and commanded by a general.

Entrance National Agency Checks (ENTNAC) The agency that checks your background to be sure you are not a security risk to the United States.

E-1, E-2, E-3, up to E-9 Pay grades. They are the same for all the armed services.

grenade A container filled with explosive material.

hitches Reenlistments.

inactive reserve After you have finished your active service, you are in the inactive reserve for the time remaining under your enlistment contract.

Initial Entry Training The first training you receive after reporting for duty.

latrines Toilets.

maneuvers A practice battle or war, involving the changing of soldiers' positions to give them the advantage over the enemy.

Military Entrance Processing Station (MEPS) The place where you take your physical, pass a security check, decide the kind of work you hope to do in the army, sign the enlistment contract and take the oath.

Military Occupational Specialty (MOS)   Skill or job specialty of a soldier.

Montgomery G.I. Bill   A Congressional bill that provides a way for soldiers to continue their education. The U.S. Army offers an enhanced G.I. Bill called the Army College Fund which can add thousands of dollars toward a college education for qualified applicants.

officer   A person who has received special training to qualify for a commission, making that person higher in rank than enlisted personnel and noncommissioned officers.

One Station Unit Training   A station (camp, post) where both basic and advanced individual training are given.

paratrooper   A soldier who, wearing a parachute, jumps from a flying aircraft.

platoon   A unit of several squads.

private (E-1)   Lowest rank in the army.

Quartermaster Corps   In charge of ordering and keeping track of supplies.

quarters   Housing.

rank   The official position or grade of a soldier.

recruit   A person who has recently joined (enlisted) in one of the armed services.

recruiter   A person who enlists new people in the armed services.

reservist   A member of a reserve unit.

Skill Qualification Test   A test of your skills required to earn a promotion.

squad   Army unit of (usually) ten people.

tour of duty   Amount of time a soldier is assigned to a specific place.

INDEX